Freddy the Frogcaster and the Huge Hurricane

By JANICE DEAN "The Weather Machine"

Illustrated by RUSS COX

Regnery® is a registered trademark of
Salem Communications Holding Corporation;
Freddy the Frogcaster™ and Regnery Kids™ are trademarks
of Salem Communications Holding Corporation.

Weather-Ready Nation Ambassador™ and the Weather-Ready Nation
Ambassador™ logo are trademarks of the U.S. Department of Commerce,
National Oceanic and Atmospheric Administration, used with permission.

Cataloging-in-Publication data on file with the
Library of Congress
ISBN 978-1-62157-260-2

Published in the United States by
Regnery Kids
An imprint of Regnery Publishing
A Division of Salem Media Group
300 New Jersey Avenue NW
Washington, DC 20001
www.RegneryKids.com

Manufactured in the United States of America
10 9 8 7 6 5 4 3 2 1

Books are available in quantity for promotional or premium use.
For information on discounts and terms, please visit our website:
www.Regnery.com.

Distributed to the trade by
Perseus Distribution
250 West 57th Street
New York, NY 10107

To Matthew and Theodore, you are my sunshine.

Freddy the Frogcaster is your Weather-Ready Nation Ambassador™,
a program of the National Oceanic and Atmospheric Administration (NOAA)

"Summer break!" Freddy cheered as the last school bell rang.

"What's your forecast for summer vacation, Freddy?" Gill Flipper asked.

"Pond-diving, frog-surfing, and lots of weather-watching!" Freddy answered. With no school, Freddy also had time to spend at the Frog News Network.

First thing the next morning, Freddy was outside checking weather clues. Light wind, low humidity, and clear blue skies...

"Perfect beach weather," Freddy said. "I hope it stays like this for our trip to the shore next week."

Meanwhile, Freddy had plenty to keep him busy. He headed back to the house for breakfast and chores.

Then Freddy was off to help Sally Croaker and Polly Woggins at the Frog News Network.

Sally welcomed Freddy with big news. "It's time for you to learn how to report the weather," she said.

"You mean on TV?" Freddy asked in a shaky voice. Weather-watching was one thing. But talking in front of a camera? That was a different story.

"Well, this is a television weather studio," Sally playfully reminded him.

"Uhh, maybe later, Sally. I'm on the lookout for hurricanes right now," Freddy said as he studied the latest satellite image.

"Uh-oh," Freddy pointed at a big swirl of clouds out in the ocean. "Is this what I think it is?"

"Let's check it out," Sally pulled up the tropical weather website. "You're right, Freddy. Hurricane hunters are investigating that cluster of storms."

Polly Woggins looked at Sally's screen. "Wind speeds are 39 miles per hour. This is the first tropical storm of the season!"

"And look," Freddy said. "It's named Andrea!"

The next day Tropical Storm Andrea was getting stronger and moving closer to land. "Look at the path of the storm," Freddy noticed. "It's heading our way!"

Polly read the weather report: "Wind speeds are up to 74 miles per hour, and the barometric pressure is dropping. That's a sure sign the storm is getting stronger. This isn't a tropical storm anymore. Andrea is now a hurricane!"

"It's time to warn everyone," Sally hopped into action and went live with a Frog News Alert. "A hurricane is making its way toward Lilypad. We need to get ready and be safe!"

Freddy hurried home to help his family. Along the way, he noticed that Lilypad was getting good at preparing for bad weather. After all, they'd had a lot of practice. First, it was a thunderstorm. Then there was the big blizzard. Now a hurricane!

"Looks like the whole town is ready, Freddy," Mr. Flyswatter
called out. "My hardware store has sold out of plywood and
flashlights."

"You're just in time to help," Freddy's dad said. "We've already put the lawn furniture away."

"The last thing we need is a lawn chair 'rocket' flying around in hurricane winds," Freddy's mom explained before heading off to the grocery store for supplies.

While his dad finished securing the windows, Freddy got busy putting together their hurricane emergency kit.

The next morning Hurricane Andrea was right on track. Winds were getting stronger. Dark clouds were rolling in. The barometric pressure was dropping even more. This huge hurricane was on the way!

Inside the news station, everyone had a job to do. Polly was going to broadcast live from outside. Sally would stay inside and report on the hurricane's path, radar, and satellite images.

"What about me?" asked Freddy.

Freddy's job was to watch the latest bulletins from the Hurricane Center and help update weather graphics.

Across town at the Frogatorium, the mayor was greeting families looking for a safe place to stay. "Welcome to the strongest building in Lilypad!" he bellowed. "We'll all be protected."

When he saw Freddy's parents, the mayor winked. "I hear Freddy's on the job. I know he won't let us down."

As Polly was outside reporting, a big gust of wind swept her off her webbed feet.

"This is Polly Woggins live outside the Frog News headquarters. Hurricane Andrea has arrived and…"

Whoosh! In an instant she was soaking wet. She hung on to a nearby sign post to steady herself.

"Yikes!" she yelled. "No frog should be out in this!"

After a while, it got really quiet outside. The wind died down and the rain tapered off.

"Whew! It's not so bad now," Polly reported.

"Polly has been out there long enough," Sally said with concern. "The eye of the storm is passing over Lilypad now. And the back side of the hurricane will hit in full force soon. I have to get her inside now!"

"But someone has to give this weather update on TV to warn all the frogs," Freddy suggested.

"You're right," Sally said and handed him the microphone. "It's time to do your first Frog News Alert, Freddy."

The words "on air" started flashing before Freddy got the chance to get scared. He stood up tall and looked right into the camera. Then he did what he had seen Sally and Polly do so many times before.

"This is Freddy the Frogcaster with breaking weather news," he said and pointed to the satellite image behind him. "This is Hurricane Andrea. The eye of the storm is right over Lilypad. It may be calm and quiet now, but don't be fooled. This hurricane isn't over yet."

Freddy cleared his throat. "Everyone needs to stay inside and be..."

"PREPARED!" Freddy's friends and family shouted. They were watching him on TV at the Frogatorium. "Go Freddy!" they cheered as their favorite young frogcaster made his television debut.

Freddy's parents were smiling proudly when the mayor hopped over. "Freddy saves the day again!" The mayor had more to say, but—whoosh—the wind howled and the rain started pounding again. The hurricane was back! Just like Freddy predicted.

Lilypad was a mess the next morning. Trees were down. Cars were flipped over. Plenty of roofs needed repair. But all that could be fixed. The good news was—everyone was safe!

Freddy was so happy to see his parents! The mayor was with them. And so was his friend Gill. "Freddy, Lilypad can't thank you enough," the mayor said, shaking Freddy's hand.

"Yes! Congratulations on your first TV report!" Gill exclaimed. "By the way, Freddy, this is for you…"

The mayor reached behind Gill's back and pulled out a long, flat package. It was tied with a big red bow.

"A frogboard for our beach trip!" Freddy said with delight. "And so far, the weather looks toad-ally awesome for surfing!"

Hi, Friends!

Whew! That hurricane was a doozy!

A hurricane is a really big ocean storm! How big? Some hurricanes measure more than 600 miles across with winds of over 200 miles per hour. I'd call that a huge hurricane, wouldn't you?

Thank goodness Lilypad's hurricane didn't get that big. But, believe me, Hurricane Andrea was big enough! After my family returned from our beach vacation (it was frogtastic!), I still had lots of questions about hurricanes. Here's what I found out:

What is a hurricane?

Some of the strongest hurricanes start in warm ocean waters near the Earth's equator. Hurricanes get their "fuel" from warm water in the ocean. As a cluster of storms comes together, the storms develop a swirling mass of powerful wind and heavy rain. In the United States and Canada (the northern hemisphere), hurricanes swirl counterclockwise around an eye in the center of the storm. In the southern hemisphere (Australia), hurricanes swirl the opposite way, or clockwise.

Hurricanes are called typhoons or cyclones in other parts of the world, even though they are the same kind of weather system.

As we found out in Lilypad, the "eye" of the hurricane is the calmest part of the storm. The eye can be anywhere from 2 miles to over 200 miles wide!

Hurricane Eye

Even though winds are quiet in the eye of the storm, the winds around the eye are usually the strongest. The eye is where the lowest surface pressures are found in the storm. Speaking of pressure, meteorologists use a barometer to measure the pressure of a hurricane. The lower the pressure, the more intense the storm is.

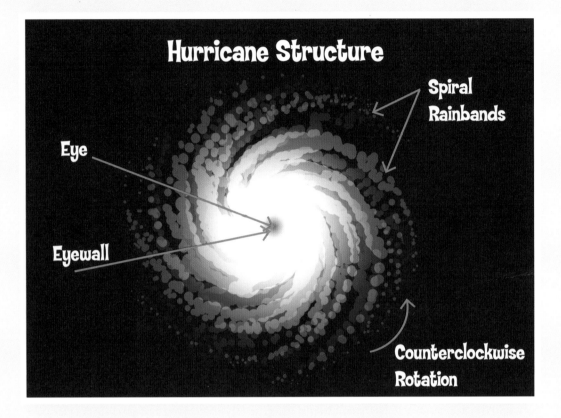

Remember how Hurricane Andrea started as a tropical storm? That's typical of hurricanes. These are the three different stages of a hurricane:

▸ A cluster of thunderstorms is called a "wave" or "disturbance" that sometimes develops into a tropical storm.

▸ If the winds measured or observed reach 39 to 73 miles per hour, the storm is classified as a tropical storm and gets its own name.

▸ If the winds bump up to at least 74 miles per hour, it's classified as a hurricane.

You can probably guess that the stronger the winds are, the more powerful the hurricane becomes. Meteorologists use a hurricane wind scale to determine how dangerous they can get.

Saffir-Simpson Hurricane Wind Scale
MPH vs. CATEGORY

74-95	**96-110**	**111-129**	**130-156**	**157+**
Some Damage	Extensive Damage	Devastating Damage	Catastrophic Damage	
CAT 1	CAT 2	CAT 3	CAT 4	CAT 5

Source: NOAA

When hurricanes come onshore (or come in contact with land), the strong winds, heavy rain, and storm surge can do a lot of damage to anything in their way including homes, roads, trees, and even coastlines.

How do people (and frogs!) know when a hurricane is coming?

The National Hurricane Center issues watches and warnings if a tropical storm or hurricane is on its way. Local news shows, radio shows, and the Internet help spread the word when a hurricane is coming.

Here's what those advisories mean:

TROPICAL STORM WATCH: Tropical storm conditions with sustained winds from 39 to 73 miles per hour are possible in your area within the next 48 hours.

TROPICAL STORM WARNING: Tropical storm conditions are expected in your area within the next 36 hours.

HURRICANE WATCH: Hurricane conditions with sustained winds of 74 miles per hour or greater are possible in your area within the next 48 hours. If you are in a hurricane watch area, your family needs to make preparations for protecting your property and decide whether or not it is a good idea to remain in your home during the hurricane. Sometimes the best place to be during a hurricane is far away!

HURRICANE WARNING: Hurricane conditions are expected in your area within 36 hours. When you hear a hurricane warning, your property should already be secured and you and your family should be in a safe place to wait out the hurricane.

What is storm surge?

The storm surge is often the most destructive part of a hurricane. Winds churn around the center of the storm, pushing in a wall of water. This wall of water gets pushed onshore and can cause major flooding and destruction.

Getting away from dangerous storm surge is why people who live along a coastal area are sometimes told to evacuate or leave their homes. We didn't have to evacuate Lilypad when Hurricane Andrea hit.

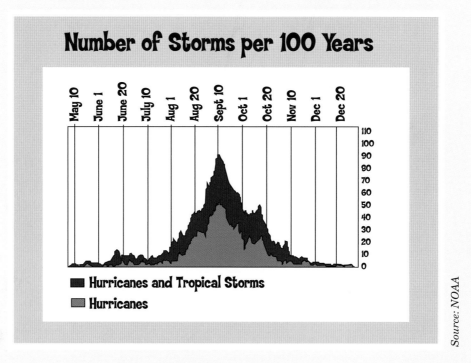

Source: NOAA

But lots of people, like my parents, went to higher ground at the Frogatorium, just to be extra safe. Of course, it's always good to know an escape route when you live in an area prone to storm surge or flooding.

The Atlantic Ocean hurricane season starts June 1 and runs until November 30. The "peak" or busiest time during hurricane season is usually in September. That means there are typically more hurricanes in September than in any of the other months.

In the eastern Pacific Ocean, hurricane season starts May 15 and ends November 30.

How do hurricanes get their names?

The hurricane that hit Lilypad was named Andrea. But real hurricanes have names too. Forecasters started "naming" hurricanes in 1953 to help identify them. The World Meteorological Organization uses different sets of names in different parts of the world. Every six years the names get rotated. So if you see a Hurricane Andrea, chances are you'll see that name pop up again in six years.

But if the storm is really, really bad, the hurricane's name is retired and replaced with something else. The names of very destructive storms like Andrew (1992), Camille (1969), Hugo (1989), Katrina (2005), and Sandy (2012) are retired and will never be used again.

What is a hurricane hunter?

Did you know that there are people who go into hurricanes to help gather data and forecast hurricanes? They are called "hurricane hunters." The hurricane hunters fly into the storm and cross back and forth to measure data like radar, temperature, air pressure, wind speed, and wind direction. And, yes, weather fans, hurricane hunters do this work INSIDE the hurricane. The crews drop instruments into the hurricane to measure the temperature, barometric pressure, and wind speeds at different levels. Hurricane hunters are awesome! They help us understand why and how these powerful storms happen.

A shrimp trawler boat damaged by Hurricane Katrina.

How can you BE PREPARED for a hurricane?

BEFORE A HURRICANE HITS: Have an emergency plan ready. Board up windows and bring in outdoor objects that could blow away. Make sure you know where all the evacuation routes are. Listen to emergency managers for possible evacuation orders.

Have a disaster supply kit for your home and car. It should include:

- A first aid kit with any medicines you take
- Canned food and a can opener
- Bottled water
- Battery-operated NOAA Weather Radio
- Flashlight
- Clothing
- If you have pets, their food and supplies

An adult in your family needs to:

- Know how to turn off electricity, gas, and water.

- Make sure your family has some money on hand since banks and ATMs may be closed.

- Be sure to fill up your car with gasoline.

DURING A HURRICANE: Stay away from low-lying and flood-prone areas. Always stay indoors during a hurricane, because strong winds will blow things around.

AFTER A HURRICANE: Stay indoors until it is safe to come out. Watch out for flooding, which can happen even after the hurricane has moved out of your area. Do not drive in flooding water. Stay away from standing water because it may be electrically charged from underground or downed power lines.

Here are some interesting facts I learned about hurricanes:

- The earliest date in the calendar year for a hurricane in the Atlantic basin was March 7, in 1908. The latest observed hurricane for the calendar year in the Atlantic basin was on December 31, in 1954.

- Mobile, Alabama, was hit by Category 3 hurricanes 10 years apart, in 1906, 1916, and 1926.

- The longest-lasting hurricane was in the Pacific Ocean. Hurricane John lasted 30 days in 1994.

- The most expensive hurricane to hit the United States was Katrina, in 2005. It caused over $100 billion in damage.

- Up to four hurricanes have been observed in the Atlantic basin at the same time.

- The letters Q, U, X, Y, and Z are not used when naming hurricanes, because there are few common names starting with these letters. Women's and men's names are alternated each year.

Here's hoping for more frog-surfing weather!

Your friend,

Freddy the Frogcaster

Acknowledgments

To Roger Ailes, thank you for giving me the world's greatest job.

To Dianne Brandi, for always keeping your door open.

To my Fox News Family for making this the best place to work.

To Brandon Noriega, who continues to keep my frogcasting and meteorological accuracy on track.

To my NOAA friends Jennifer Sprague and Doug Hilderbrand. Our Freddy is "Weather-Ready"!

To Tom Champoux, my AMS friend, for brain "storming" ideas for future Freddy adventures.

To Russ Cox, my brilliant illustrator. Don't ever leave me.

To my support team at Regnery Kids—Cheryl Barnes, Marji Ross, Mark Bloomfield, Matthew Maschino, Diane Reeves, Emily Bruce, and Maria Ruhl.

To all of the children, parents, grandparents, teachers, and librarians who have read Freddy out loud in classrooms and at home across the country. You never know when we might inspire our next generation of meteorologists! I am TOAD-ALLY honored.

And to Sean. Seasons will always change, but our love continues to grow deeper each year. Thank you for being the best husband and father I've ever known.

Enjoy more of Freddy's weather adventures in

ISBN: 978-1-62157-084-4   ISBN: 978-1-62157-254-1